Malcolm was a young boy wi[th a lot]
of energy and curiosity. He was kn[own thr]oughout
the neighborhood as the liveliest and most
adventurous child around.

He never missed a time to have fun
with his best friend, Umar.

One chilly morning, Malcolm woke up with
a yawn and stretched his arms high above his head.

He glanced out the window and saw
the world covered in a thick layer of snow.

"Brr, looks like a snow day," he muttered to himself, rubbing his eyes sleepily.

But as he looked around his room, he couldn't shake off the feeling of boredom creeping in.

"Ugh, being stuck indoors is so boring,"
Malcolm complained, flopping back onto his
bed with a dramatic sigh. "I need some action!"

So after breakfast, Malcolm asked his parents,
"Mommy, daddy, can I go play outside?"

"Sure you can, but just remember, stay away from the sneaky snow bunnies! They're dangerous!" his mom warned with a serious tone.

"Okay," Malcolm said, his eyes wide with curiosity as he skipped out the door to find his best friend.

He found Umar playing with his toy truck in the snow, and as soon as Umar saw him, he ran over, breathing heavily.

"Malcolm, I've been looking for you all day!"
Umar exclaimed. "It's the sneaky snow bunnies!
They won't leave me alone! Every time I get my
allowance, they try to trick me into
giving them my money."

Malcolm frowned as he remembered what his mom had told him. "That's not right!"

"I know. Let's go play, but keep a close eye on those sneaky snow bunnies," Umar suggested as they set off to play.

As Malcolm and Umar built a snow fort, a sneaky snow bunny approached them with a sly grin on its face. "What do you want, sneaky snow bunny?" Umar asked cautiously.

The bunny looked innocent. "There's a carrot stuck under the fence down the street. Would one of you strong gentlemen help me pull it out?"

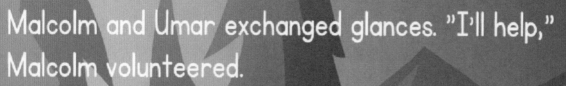

Malcolm and Umar exchanged glances. "I'll help,"
Malcolm volunteered.
"No, Malcolm! We must stay focused! Remember
what your parents said?" Umar warned, looking nervous.
"It's okay, Umar. I'll be right back," Malcolm said, heading
confidently towards the fence.

However, as soon as he reached for the carrot, more snow bunnies appeared. In the blink of an eye, one bunny snatched his gloves, another took his coat, and a third hopped away with his money. They ran off into the forest, leaving Malcolm stunned and shivering in the cold.

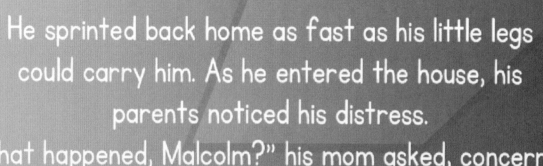

He sprinted back home as fast as his little legs
could carry him. As he entered the house, his
parents noticed his distress.
"What happened, Malcolm?" his mom asked, concerned.
"It was the snow bunnies. They tricked me,"
Malcolm confessed, lowering his head.
"She... she said she needed help getting a carrot,
but they only wanted to take all of my belongings."

His parents exchanged knowing glances. "We love you, Malcolm, but there's a reason we warned you about those snow bunnies. They lie to get anything they want. It's important that you always listen to your parents."

Malcolm hugged his parents tightly.
"I'm sorry, Mom and Dad, for not listening. I'll
never trust another snow bunny ever again."

Later that day, Malcolm's grandpa came to visit, carrying a mysterious bag. "Malcolm, I have a surprise for you!" he exclaimed. Malcolm's eyes lit up as his grandpa reached into the bag and handed him his gloves, coat, and some money.

"Grandpa, how did you get my clothes and money back?" Malcolm asked in a surprised voice.

"I heard about what happened, so I went to where the snow bunnies hang out. I learned never to trust sneaky snow bunnies a long time ago," grandpa explained. "My father and mother warned me just like yours, but I didn't listen either. I hope you learned your lesson, my boy."

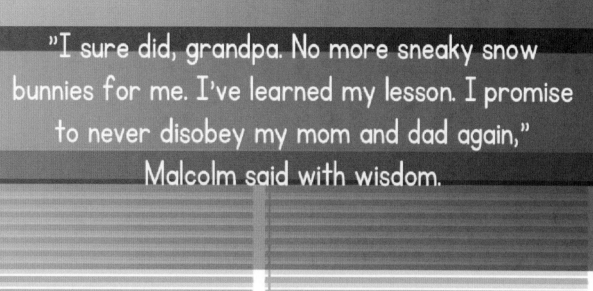

"I sure did, grandpa. No more sneaky snow bunnies for me. I've learned my lesson. I promise to never disobey my mom and dad again," Malcolm said with wisdom.

And so, Malcolm continued to play happily,
making sure to always listen to his parents
and stay away from the mischievous snow bunnies.
The lessons he learned that day stayed with him
throughout his life, ensuring he never fell for
the tricks of sneaky creatures again.

Made in the USA
Middletown, DE
18 February 2024

50009392R00015